← **YOU CHOOSE** →

SCOOBY-DOO!™

THE SECRET OF THE SEA CREATURE

Stone Arch Books
A Capstone Imprint

You Choose Stories: Scooby-Doo
is published by Stone Arch Books,
A Capstone Imprint
1710 Roe Crest Drive
North Mankato, Minnesota 56003
www.capstonepub.com

Cataloging-in-Publication Data is available on the
Library of Congress website.
ISBN: 978-1-4342-6404-6 [Library Hardcover]
ISBN: 978-1-4342-7925-5 [Paperback]

Summary: Scooby-Doo and the gang need your
help solving the secret of the sea creature
in this You Choose mystery!

Printed in the United States of America in Stevens Point, Wisconsin.
092013   007765WZS14

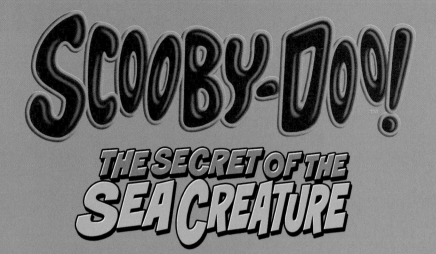

SCOOBY-DOO!
THE SECRET OF THE SEA CREATURE

written by
Laurie S. Sutton

illustrated by
Scott Neely

THE MYSTERY INC. GANG!

SCOOBY-DOO

SKILLS: Loyal; super snout
BIO: This happy-go-lucky hound avoids scary situations at all costs, but he'll do anything for a Scooby Snack!

SHAGGY ROGERS

SKILLS: Lucky; healthy appetite
BIO: This laid-back dude would rather look for grub than search for clues, but he usually finds both!

FRED JONES, JR.

SKILLS: Athletic; charming
BIO: The leader and oldest member of the gang. He's a good sport—and good at them, too!

DAPHNE BLAKE

SKILLS: Brains; beauty
BIO: As a sixteen-year-old fashion queen, Daphne solves her mysteries in style.

VELMA DINKLEY

SKILLS: Clever; highly intelligent
BIO: Although she's the youngest member of Mystery Inc., Velma's an old pro at catching crooks.

← YOU CHOOSE →

SCOOBY-DOO!

A sea creature is on the loose at **Wild-World Beach!** Only YOU can help Scooby-Doo and the Mystery Inc. gang solve this maritime mystery.

Follow the directions at the bottom of each page. The choices YOU make will change the outcome of the story. After you finish one path, go back and read the others for more Scooby-Doo adventures!

YOU CHOOSE the path to solve...

THE SECRET OF THE SEA CREATURE

On a hot, steamy day, the Mystery Machine zooms down the highway. Fred Jones, Jr. is at the wheel of the lime-green van. He's the leader of Mystery Inc., a gang of teenage crime solvers, but today is all about summer fun.

"What a great day for a drive to the beach!" says Daphne from the passenger seat.

"Like, are we there yet?" Shaggy moans.

"Ryeah, are we rhere yet?" Scooby-Doo whimpers from the back seat. "Ri'm hungry!"

"You guys are always hungry," Velma points out, pushing her glasses up her nose. "You don't have stomachs. You two have bottomless pits!"

Turn the page.

"Aw, Velma," Shaggy replies. "Like, we just can't wait to taste those famous Wild-World Beach hot dogs. Right, boy?"

"Ryeah! Rummy!" says Scooby, licking his lips. Drool drips from the dog's long, wagging tongue.

"Well, you can eat all the hot dogs you want," Velma says. "I'm more interested in the rare shells." She pulls out a book about seashells.

"Yuck! I don't like snails," Shaggy exclaims.

"Not snails—shells!" Velma says. "Wild-World Beach is home to the *Conus beautificus*, also known as the Jewel of the Sea." She opens her book to a picture of the rainbow-colored shell.

"Yeah, and it's also a great place to snorkel," Fred adds, glancing back at them in the rearview mirror. "That's what I'm going to do!"

"I didn't know you liked to snorkel, Fred," says Daphne.

"Oh, sure," Fred replies with a proud grin. "I'm an all-round sports-type dude."

"What are you going to do at Wild-World, Daphne?" Velma asks.

"I'm going hunting," Daphne replies.

"WHAT?!" the gang shouts together. Fred is so surprised he nearly drives off the road.

"Like, lions, tigers, and bears, and stuff?" Shaggy says with a loud gulp.

"Rhose poor rittle ranimals!" Scooby-Doo whimpers, covering his eyes with a paw.

Daphne shows them a flashy magazine, which is filled with dozens of photographs of celebrities and other famous people on the cover. "Not animal hunting, silly. Celebrity hunting!" she explains. "I read that movie stars like to go to this beach. Maybe I can meet one."

"Rhew!" exclaims Scooby, relieved.

Turn the page.

Just then, the Mystery Machine drives past a road sign that points to the exit for Wild-World Beach and Amusement Park.

"We're here!" Shaggy says. "I can almost smell those foot-long hot dogs with all the fixings."

"Rippeee!" Scooby-Doo agrees. His snout twitches wildly. "I smell rhem right now!"

Scooby's legs spin like pinwheels as he gets ready to run. Fred barely has enough time to drive the van onto the exit before Shaggy and Scooby-Doo are out the door and down the road.

"I guess we'll meet them there," says Velma.

Fred parks the Mystery Machine not far from the beach. The gang climbs out of the van and looks around. The beach is jam-packed with people. Kids are with their moms and dads. A group plays volleyball. Friends toss a football. Everyone is having fun.

They can see the rides in the amusement park and the kite surfers on the water. They don't see Shaggy or Scooby-Doo, but that doesn't worry them. Those two chowhounds are easy to find— just look for a food stand!

"I'm off to search for shells," Velma says.

"And I'm going kitesurfing," adds Daphne.

The two girls head toward the beach.

"Okay, let's split up for now," Fred suggests, jogging toward the surf.

To follow Velma, turn to page 12.

To follow Shaggy & Scooby, turn to page 13.

To follow Daphne, turn to page 14.

To follow Fred, turn to page 16.

Leaving the Mystery Inc. gang, Velma walks along the beach, searching for the Jewel of the Sea. With her head down, she concentrates on finding one of the rare shells. But she doesn't see anything except sand. "Not many shells on the beach today," she says with a heavy sigh.

Suddenly, Velma hears shouting. *Did someone say "shark"?* she wonders.

Then, a nearby lifeguard warns people to get out of the water. *WEEEEEE!* He blows his whistle urgently. Velma looks up from her seashell search and sees people running from the beach.

A huge creature bursts up out of the surf like a powerful geyser. Velma quickly realizes that it's not a shark. It's much bigger and much more dangerous. It's a sea monster!

If Velma decides to take a closer look, turn to page 18.
If Velma waits on the beach for help, turn to page 63.

Away from the gang, Scooby-Doo and his
best pal, Shaggy, quickly gulp down Wild-World
Beach's famous hot dogs.

"It's dog-eat-dog, if you know what I mean,
Scoob!" says Shaggy, chuckling.

"Ryeah!" Scooby agrees. "Ri never met a rog
Ri didn't rike."

The friends lick their lips with big sloppy
tongues. They don't need napkins. Every trace of
ketchup, mustard, relish, onions, pickles, cheese,
and chili is gone in a single swipe!

"Row about rotton candy?" Scooby suggests.

"Like, there's nothing better than spun sugar
on a stick!" Shaggy says. "Let's go!"

Hurrying along the pier, they suddenly hear a
burst of screaming!

If Shaggy & Scooby ignore the screams, turn to page 20.
If Shaggy & Scooby investigate the screams, turn to page 99.

After leaving the gang, Daphne rents a kiteboard and heads into the ocean. She zips across the surface of the water on her board as fast as the breeze can carry her. Daphne jumps and twists in the air, then lands with a splash.

SPA-LOOSH!

The bow-shaped sail above her head pulls Daphne parallel to the shore. She tries to look for celebrities on the beach as she surfs, but she's too busy controlling the kite.

"Maybe I should have stayed on land," Daphne says. "Besides, the sea spray is ruining my hair and makeup."

Suddenly, Daphne hears the lifeguard blow his whistle frantically. *What is he shouting?* she wonders, unable to hear him clearly.

"Why is everyone running off the beach?" she asks herself. "Am I missing something exciting?"

Daphne turns her kiteboard around to sail toward shore. That's when she sees what everyone is yelling about. A giant sea monster rises out of the water right in front of her!

"Jeepers!" Daphne exclaims.

The wind blows Daphne's kite straight toward the monster. She pulls on the lines and tries to turn her board.

Then, a strong gust catches the billowing sail and lifts Daphne high into the air. She is at the mercy of the sea breeze. The monster reaches out with its giant tentacles and tries to grab her.

"If this creepy creature catches me, I'm in real trouble!" Daphne says.

If Daphne lowers the kiteboard to the water, turn to page 24.
If Daphne lifts her kiteboard higher in the sky, turn to page 51.

After leaving the gang, Fred snorkels along an artificial reef. At first he floats on the surface and watches the fish swim among the plants and rocks. They are all the colors of the rainbow! Then Fred takes a deep breath and dives.

This is better than any aquarium! Fred thinks. *I could reach out and touch the fish—if they didn't swim so fast!*

Right then, something silvery catches his attention. It resembles a bright eel swimming through the water like a weightless snake. Fred has never seen anything like it, so he follows the unusual creature. It disappears into a crack in the reef.

Fred puts his face mask up to the crevice to look inside. A giant eyeball looks back!

Fred is so startled that he instinctively shouts under water. He exhales and all the breath leaves his lungs. Fred is forced to surface.

"What was that?" he says as he floats on top of the water. "I've got to investigate!"

Fred inhales an extra-deep breath this time. He dives back down to the reef. When he gets to the crack, he boldly peers inside. Nothing looks back at him.

Did I imagine it? Fred questions himself. *It seemed so real.*

Suddenly, something gigantic rises up out of the reef. It has silvery skin just like the eel and tentacles like a squid.

I didn't imagine anything. I saw a real sea monster! Fred realizes.

Turn to page 26.

Velma drops her stash of seashells and heads toward the water for a closer look. She isn't afraid of sea monsters. She and the Mystery Inc. gang are experts of the weird and mysterious.

"There's an explanation for everything!" Velma exclaims, creeping closer and closer to the strange, aquatic beast.

Suddenly, one of the monster's tentacles grabs Velma and lifts her high into the air. It shakes her so hard that her glasses almost fall off.

Velma is worried. "I can't see anything without my glasses!" she cries out.

The sea monster's tentacle has Velma in its grasp. *WHOOSH! WHOOSH!* It whips her in circles, around and around its head.

Moments later, Velma is right in front of its eyeball! She notices this is no ordinary eyeball. There's a man inside! He's in a control room.

"This monster is man-made," Velma realizes. "There *is* an explanation for everything!"

Velma wonders if she should try to escape from the mechanical monster's clutches. *If I struggle, the sea monster's controller might get even more upset,* she thinks.

She considers shouting for help instead. Maybe someone will save her in time.

If Velma tries to escape on her own, turn to page 29.
If Velma shouts for help, turn to page 38.

Shaggy and Scooby-Doo have their taste buds set on cotton candy. People are screaming, but the pals pay no attention. It's the sound of people having fun on the rides, right?

Suddenly, a mob thunders over Scooby and Shaggy. People are in a panic!

Whoa! What's the rush? Shaggy wonders as a hundred heels pummel him. He looks for his canine friend, but he can't find him in the throng. "Scooby-Doo, where are you?"

"Rhere Ri am!" Scooby replies. He pops up with an ice cream cone, a corn dog, and a slice of pizza in his paws. "Rummy!"

"Like, where's everybody going? Did a new food stand open?" Shaggy asks, confused.

"Ruh-ruh-ruh roh!" Scooby-Doo stutters. "Rat's rhy! Rook!"

Scooby points with his paw.

Turn to page 22.

Shaggy stares down the beach and sees what Scooby is pointing at.

A giant eyeball stares down at them, and it belongs to an even bigger sea monster! Thick tentacles grip and crush the vendor stands as the creature crawls along the boardwalk.

There's only one thing Shaggy and Scooby-Doo can do!

"Zoinks!" says Shaggy. "Like, run, Scoobs!"

WHOOSH!

The two friends take off in a flash. They flee so fast that they don't have time to think—what's a sea monster doing on land? The only thing on their minds is escape!

Scooby and Shaggy are so frazzled they don't think straight. They don't follow the rest of the crowd running away from the monster. They run in the opposite direction!

The monster chases them into the nearby amusement park.

"He's after us!" Shaggy yells. "Faster, Scoobs! We need to outrun this crazy creature!"

Scooby-Doo shakes his head like a wet dog. "Ride! Ride!" he suggests instead.

If Shaggy & Scooby find a place to hide, turn to page 68.

If Shaggy & Scooby keep running, turn to page 94.

Daphne lowers her kiteboard to the water below, but she can't escape the sea monster. The kite gets tangled in the sea monster's extra-long tentacles. They whip her around and around until she is dizzy.

To make matters worse, a swarm of police and Coast Guard helicopters buzz the monster. It swats at them with its tentacles, including the ones that have Daphne snared.

"This is going to give me whiplash," Daphne says. "I have to get myself out of this. But how?"

WHOOSH! Another strong gust of wind fills Daphne's kite. The fabric billows. The nylon lines pull at Daphne's harness. The kite pulls the sea monster sideways, too. It isn't very much, but it gives Daphne an idea!

"Those helicopters will come in handy," she says. Daphne waves at them to come closer. "Help! Help! Save me from this monster!"

THWOOP! THWOOP! THWOOP!

A large Coast Guard chopper soars toward Daphne. She can see a rescue diver in the open hatch and feel the buffeting wind caused by the turning rotors. The canopy of Daphne's sail swells, and the monster is dragged along behind it like a kitesurfer.

But Daphne's not safe yet. The monster is heading for a sea cliff!

Turn to page 33.

Fred can't resist the temptation to reach out and touch the sea monster. He is surprised to discover that its skin isn't skin at all. It's plastic! He pinches the monster. It doesn't react.

Well, what do you know? This monster is a machine! Fred concludes. *That's a relief.*

Suddenly, the water churns as the monster starts to swim away from the reef. Fred grabs onto one of the tentacles. He wants to find out who is behind this maritime menace.

Fred worries. *I just hope I can hold my breath long enough to solve this mystery!*

If Fred is carried out to sea, turn to page 27.
If Fred is carried deeper under water, turn to page 40.

The monster carries Fred out to sea. It travels at a tremendous speed. Fred can barely hold on, and he is running out of breath!

If I let go now, I'm doomed! Fred thinks. *I must be in the middle of the ocean. No one will ever find me.*

Suddenly, he sees a brilliant light in the distance. It's a submarine beacon. It guides the mechanical monster toward a massive underwater building. The monster slows down as it approaches.

Don't put on the brakes now! I'm about to turn blue! Fred thinks. His lungs burn from lack of air.

The monster swims into the building. Fred swims to the surface and sees that he is in a large docking bay. There are small submarines and other underwater vessels all around the large chamber.

Turn the page.

None of them have any identifying marks. That makes Fred suspicious. When he sees armed guards patrolling up and down the docks, he knows something serious is happening here.

"Who are these people and what are they doing here?" he wonders. "Are they smugglers? Pirates? Spies?"

Fred swims over to a ladder. He wants to look around and figure out this mystery. He doesn't get far before one of the guards sees him.

"Halt!" the guard shouts.

Fred does just the opposite. He runs!

Turn to page 46.

"I have to escape and tell the authorities that this monster is a fake," Velma says.

She tries to break free from the monster's grasp, but it's as tight as a vice.

"It's too strong," Velma realizes. "But I'll bet my brains are better than its brawn."

Thinking fast, Velma takes off her glasses and points them toward the bright, midday sun. The polished lenses reflect the light right through the mechanical monster's eye sockets.

The beam floods the machine's high-tech control room. The man inside is blinded by the light streaming in.

"Ahhh!" the man yells. He covers his eyes with his hands to block the dazzling glare.

The man inside the monster takes his hands off the controls for a split second.

Turn to page 31.

Immediately, the mechanical tentacle releases Velma. Her trick worked! She drops into the water with a big splash. *SPLOOOSH!*

Suddenly, a Coast Guard boat speeds up to her. They've come to rescue her.

"That's not a real sea monster," Velma tells the crewmembers. "That's a machine. A man inside is controlling it."

The Coast Guard officers take Velma to a larger ship. She tells its commander what she told her rescuers: the monster is a fake.

"Fire the nets!" shouts the commander.

The Coast Guard ship fires its net cannon at the fake sea monster.

BOOM! BOOM! Giant nets explode from the ship's cannons and tangle around the monster. Struggling to get free, its head breaks off and floats on the surface, then it starts to sink.

Turn the page.

32

"Look! There's the man who was controlling the monster!" Velma says. She points at him swimming near the sinking head.

The Coast Guard sends a boat to pull the man out of the water and arrest him. When he is brought back to the ship, he sees Velma.

"You meddling girl!" he shouts. "I built that sea monster to scare kids like you off this beach. It used to be my favorite fishing spot! And I would have succeeded if it weren't for you."

"I hear that a lot," Velma says. She can't wait to tell Scooby and the gang about what she found on her seashell search.

THE END

To follow another path, turn to page 11.

The sea monster is going to smash against the sea cliff! Daphne is still tangled in the tentacles. She can't get out of her harness.

"This is not how I planned to spend my day at the beach," Daphne says.

Suddenly, a hatch opens in the body of the sea monster. A woman looks up at Daphne and scowls at her just before jumping into the water.

"Well, what do you know? The monster is fake. Typical," Daphne says.

The Coast Guard rescue diver drops down on a cable from the helicopter and hangs next to Daphne. He cuts her kite harness and frees her from the doomed monster. Seconds later, it smashes into the cliff and explodes. *KA-BOOM!*

The Coast Guard helicopter lands on the beach and Daphne jumps out. Reporters and TV news crews quickly surround her. They all want to hear how she stopped the sea monster.

Turn the page.

Daphne takes off her kiteboarding helmet and fluffs her hair. She wants to look good for the cameras and onlookers.

"You meddling kid! You ruined my publicity stunt!" the woman from inside the monster yells as nearby police handcuff her. "Those reporters should be talking to me, not you!"

"Hey, Daphne, what did we miss?" Fred asks. He and the rest of the Mystery Inc. gang join her on the beach.

"Oh, nothing new," Daphne says with a shrug. "A fake monster. A daring rescue. Same old thing." She turns to the waiting reporters and winks.

"Yeah, sounds pretty normal," Shaggy agrees. "Hey, Scoobs, let's get something to eat!"

THE END

To follow another path, turn to page 11.

Shaggy drops from the monster's grip and falls into the water.

"Hey, Scooby! Who knew your taste for sushi would save us?" Shaggy says. He looks around for his pal. "Scooby-Doo! Where are you?"

"Rup here," Scooby says from above. He is hanging from the tentacle. "Ri'm ruck!"

The tentacle tries to fling Scooby loose, but he's stuck like glue. All the shaking makes him hang on harder than ever! His eyes rattle in his head, and he starts to see double. All of a sudden Scooby is loose. He soars through the air.

SPLAT! Scooby lands against the monster's eyeball.

"Yuck!" Shaggy cringes when he watches Scooby slide down the eye.

"Hey, rit's plastic," Scooby-Doo says. "And rhere's a guy rinside!"

Turn the page.

Scooby drops into the water near Shaggy. He doggie paddles over to his friend.

"Like, am I glad to see you, pal!" Shaggy says. "You sure had a mouthful of trouble!"

"And rit rasted rerrible!" Scooby agrees.

"That guy and his fake monster are ruining everyone's day at the beach," Shaggy says. "I think it's time we ruined his."

"Ryeah!" Scooby agrees. But then he stops. "Uh, *re*?"

"I have a great idea! Come on!" Shaggy says and swims toward the beach.

"Ruh-roh," Scooby worries, but he follows his friend.

Shaggy and Scooby go to the deserted amusement park. Everyone has run to safety. There is no one to stop the pals from climbing into the park's giant robot mascot.

"Do rou know row to work ris?" Scooby asks.

"Like, how hard can it be?" Shaggy replies. He pushes a few buttons.

The machine staggers toward the beach with Shaggy at the controls. It smashes the lifeguard tower and a few food stands along the way.

WHAM! BANG! SMASH!

"Oops!" Shaggy says. "Like, this is why I let Fred drive the Mystery Machine."

"Rook rout!" Scooby warns. A giant tentacle whips toward the mascot.

"Maybe this wasn't such a good idea," Shaggy admits. The tentacle grabs the mascot. "Zoinks! We're doomed!"

Turn to page 87.

"Help!" Velma decides to shout.

Beachgoers splash out of the water and scramble onto shore, away from the sea monster. No one hears Velma's cries—except the man at the monster's high-tech controls.

"That meddling girl spotted me!" the man shouts. "I can't let her tell anyone."

The man angrily yanks on the controls of the mechanical monster. Immediately, the tentacle holding Velma moves toward the monster's body. A hatch opens! Velma is tossed inside the mechanical monster, and the hatch slams shut.

At first everything is very dark, but soon Velma's eyes adjust, and she can see her surroundings. There are steel beams and sheets of metal on the floor, ceiling, and walls.

"This looks like the inside of the Statue of Liberty," Velma says. "Only this one moves!"

Velma searches frantically for a way out. The hatch is sealed shut. Two other doors—one to her left and one to her right—can be seen inside the mechanical monster.

"Hmm, I wonder where these doors lead?" Velma says. Slowly, she reaches out her hand to grab the left door handle.

Then, Velma stops.

"One or both of these doors could be booby-trapped," Velma decides. "If I invented a mechanical sea monster, I'd set a trap on entrances into my invention."

Velma thinks about what to do next. She decides to take a chance on one of the doors!

If Velma chooses the right door, turn to page 49.
If Velma chooses the left door, turn to page 102.

Fred is carried deeper and deeper under water. He doesn't dare let go. It's too far to the surface. The water is getting dark around him. He's being carried beyond the sunlight zone.

I don't think I can hold my breath much longer! Fred worries. *I'm starting to see spots before my eyes.*

The spots glimmer like stars. Then Fred realizes that he's seeing sparkling metal. The monster is pulling him toward a flying saucer resting on the sea floor!

Sea monsters and aliens?! Fred wonders in amazement. *The lack of oxygen must be affecting my brain . . .*

Turn to page 42.

The monster swims through a hatch in the spaceship. There is light and air inside. Fred comes to the surface and gasps for breath. He is in a docking area. Other sea monsters are moored close by.

Then Fred sees the aliens! They are humanoid and have big round heads with multiple eyes. "I hope they come in peace," Fred says. Then he sees they have weapons. "Well, maybe not."

Suddenly one of the aliens removes its head! It turns out to be a human wearing a diving helmet. The eyes are actually window slits.

"The aliens are as fake as the sea monster," Fred concludes. "But what are they up to? Why do they need such an elaborate disguise?"

Fred knows it's time to investigate this mystery.

Turn to page 95.

Shaggy and Scooby decide to let go of the ride. They soar through the air and land on the top of a tall waterslide. The carousel and the sea monster are far below them.

"That was close!" Shaggy says. "We're safe up here, Scoobs. Sea monsters can't climb stairs."

"Ris one can!" Scooby-Doo barks. He points to the monster. It's using its tentacles to climb to the top of the slide.

"That's some sea monster!" Shaggy exclaims. "There's only one thing to do, Scoob."

"What?" Scooby asks.

"Jump!" Shaggy replies, leaping onto the waterslide.

"Scooby Dooby Doo!" Scooby yells and follows his pal.

Shaggy and Scooby-Doo slip down the waterslide to escape the sea monster.

Turn the page.

They barely miss being grabbed by a tentacle.

"Yaaaa!" the pals yell as they plunge down a steep drop. To their surprise, the sea monster follows them!

"It's gaining on us!" Shaggy shouts. The monster speeds toward them like a torpedo.

"Rook out for the roops!" warns Scooby.

Shaggy and Scooby hang on to each other as they go through the waterslide's upside-down loops. They go up, down, and around again. So does the monster. They all land in the giant splash pool at the end of the ride.

Shaggy and Scooby scramble out of the water. But the monster doesn't move!

ZAP! CRACKLE! POP!

Sparks fly out of the sinister sea monster. Its eight tentacles are broken. They are made of metal and wires.

"Like, it's a machine!" Shaggy realizes. "The water shorted out its circuits."

"Rom rea monster," Scooby says.

Suddenly, one of the monster's eyeballs pops open. It's an escape hatch. A man crawls out, and the awaiting police arrest him immediately.

"You meddling kid!" he shouts at Shaggy and Scooby-Doo. "I wanted to scare people away from the park and buy the land to turn it into condos. I would have gotten away with it if it hadn't been for you and your goofy dog!"

"Rey! Who's roofy?" Scooby asks.

"Let's go find something to eat, Scoobs," Shaggy says. "I don't want to tell this story to the gang on an empty stomach."

THE END

To follow another path, turn to page 11.

The guard chases Fred through the strange facility.

Fred ducks through a doorway and quickly shuts the door behind him. He's in inky, pitch-black darkness. Right now that doesn't worry him, though. He's more concerned about hearing if the guard runs past his hiding place.

Fred presses his ear against the door.

"Why is the door soft?" he wonders aloud. *SNIFF! SNIFF!* "What's that smell?"

Fred gropes along the wall until he finds a light switch. When he turns on the lights, he sees wet suits and diving equipment hanging on the back of the door and on every wall. The smell is from damp suits and swim fins.

"These suits smell awful, but they'll come in handy," Fred decides.

"I can use these as a disguise," Fred says.

"Then I can look around this underwater headquarters and find out what's up," he adds.

Fred tries to pull on a pair of the leggings. They are a tight fit, and the damp material grabs his skin. He wiggles and jumps and strains until he gets the pants on at last. He reaches for one of the short-sleeved tops and starts to put it on over his head.

CREAAAKKK!

Suddenly the door opens!

"Who's in here?" a voice demands.

Fred has the wet suit top halfway over his head. He can't see who has opened the door.

"Sam, is that you?" the voice asks.

"Uh, no, it's Fred," Fred replies. "Sam is on a break."

"Uh, okay," the voice says. "Thanks."

Turn the page.

Fred listens to the door close. He quickly pulls the wet suit top over his head and looks around. There is no one in the room with him.

Fred sighs in relief. He goes to the door and peers outside. The hallway is empty.

He is safe—for now.

"That was close!" Fred says.

Turn to page 70.

Velma grabs the door handle on the right.

ZAPPP!

"Jeepers!" Velma exclaims. "That door is electrified!"

It's only a mild shock, but it's enough to stop Velma from touching the other handle.

Velma searches every inch of the metal room, but there are no other exits. No window or trapdoor or air vent.

"It looks like I'm trapped in here," Velma decides. She isn't afraid. "If I know Scooby-Doo and the gang, they'll investigate this monster and find out it's fake. I'll be rescued soon."

Velma sits down on the cold metal floor to wait for the other Mystery Inc. members.

THE END

To follow another path, turn to page 11.

Daphne pulls on the kite's lines as hard as she can, lifting the kiteboard higher in the sky. She banks away from the monster. Daphne is safe from the maritime menace, but she's not out of danger. The wind gust carries her even higher into the air. She flies like a bird!

"Jeepers! I'm not heavy enough to make my kite drop," Daphne realizes. "I guess my diet really worked!"

Daphne worries that a shift in the wind could carry her out to sea or into a sea cliff. She could collide with one of the helicopters flying around the sea monster.

"Or, that flock of seagulls could hit me!" Daphne says to herself.

A cloud of seabirds flies toward Daphne. The sea monster and the noisy helicopters have frightened them. Daphne swerves her kite to avoid them, but she can't get out of the way.

Turn the page.

The birds strike Daphne and her sail. Even though she's wearing a protective vest and helmet, Daphne feels like huge hailstones are hitting her. She and the kiteboard take a beating.

Then she hears a sound that sends a bolt of fear down her spine.

RIIIIP!

"Oh, no! The birds shredded my kite!" Daphne realizes. "I'm going to crash!"

Turn to page 88.

Fred manages to find his way back to the docking bay. It takes him a long time. All the hallways look the same!

"I need a plan of escape," Fred says to himself. He looks around the docks and sees the mechanical sea monster moored nearby. "I know! I'll just leave the same way I arrived."

Fred starts to walk across the dock toward the monster. No one notices him. He is almost at his goal when alarms begin to blare. Everyone on the docks runs—including Fred!

Fred sprints toward the sea monster.

The mechanical monster is not guarded. Fred jumps into the control pod through the open eyeball hatch.

"Made it! Now how does this thing work?" Fred asks himself. "First things first—how do I close the hatch?"

Turn the page.

Fred presses buttons at random. Engines switch on, tentacles thrash, and the eyeball hatch lowers. Suddenly, a powerful concussion pounds the underwater base!

KA-BOOM!

Everyone on the docks falls down. They are all knocked unconscious.

"Um, did I do that?" Fred wonders aloud.

Fred studies the control panel of the sea monster. "Hey, this is as easy as driving the Mystery Machine!" he says. A few minutes later Fred gets the sea monster to the surface.

But he is surrounded by Navy ships.

"Surrender or be captured," a voice is heard over a loudspeaker.

"They don't know I'm one of the good guys!" Fred realizes. "It's time to abandon ship—um, monster!"

Fred leaps from the machine just as it is captured by a gigantic net. He swims away and is plucked out of the water by the Coast Guard.

"Put your hands up!" the officer commands.

Turn to page 78.

Velma is safe behind the large granite rock with her friends. She studies the sea monster threatening the beach. All the people have run away in fear.

Velma isn't afraid. She's curious.

"That's not a sea monster," Velma says. "A creature that shape and size can't live at the surface of the ocean. Not a real one, anyway."

Velma stands up from the shelter of the rock.

"Even a giant squid can't do what that thing is doing," Velma says. "That monster is a fake!"

"Velma's right," Fred says. He shouts to the people on the beach. "Hey, everyone! The monster is a phony!"

"Here, we'll prove it!" Daphne yells.

She throws a rock at the monster. It makes a metallic sound as it bounces off the creature.

Turn to page 58.

The people on the beach realize that they've been tricked. Everyone picks up a pebble, a seashell, or a piece of litter and throws it at the sea monster!

DING! PING! The objects hit metal.

"Those kids are right!" someone yells. "It's a fake! Get it!"

Moments later, a helicopter lands on the beach between the crowd and the sea monster. A movie director jumps out.

"You meddling kids ruined my monster movie!" he shouts. "I wanted to film real people reacting to a sea monster."

"Like, I think you might want to rewrite the ending," Shaggy says as the police rush in to arrest the man.

THE END

To follow another path, turn to page 11.

Scooby-Doo leaps off the pier and into the water with Shaggy. They make a big splash. Suddenly, there's an even bigger splash. The sea monster has jumped into the water, too!

"Swim!" Shaggy shouts. Scooby doggie paddles as fast as he can. A large wave catches the two pals. "Surf's up!"

The wave carries Shaggy and Scooby toward a sea cave. It's dark and scary, but the sea monster swimming after them is even scarier! They hope they can hide from it inside the cave.

A current drags Shaggy and Scooby-Doo deep into the cavern. They float into a large chamber. There are bright veins of ore in the walls.

"Like, it's a mine!" Shaggy says. "A gold mine!"

The sea monster rises out of the water inside the cave. Shaggy and Scooby climb onto a rock ledge, trying to get away. There is no escape.

Turn the page.

"It's been nice knowing you, Scoobs," Shaggy says, sobbing.

"So rong, ral," Scooby whimpers.

Seconds later, a window pops open in one of the monster's eyeballs and a man leans out. Shaggy and Scooby look at each other in surprise.

"Like, the monster is a machine?" Shaggy exclaims.

"It's a Mining Operations Commercial Krushing Octopod, or M.O.C.K. Ock for short," the man states. "But you two aren't going to live to tell anyone about it!"

The mechanical monster raises its tentacles to smash Scooby-Doo and Shaggy. They hug each other and shiver. This is it! They're doomed.

Turn to page 62.

Suddenly, there is a huge crash as the tentacles hit the ceiling of the mine. Rocks start falling on the fake monster. The whole roof collapses! Shaggy and Scooby are safe on the rock ledge. When the dust clears, the monster is buried under a pile of rubble.

Soon, police arrive to investigate the mysterious rockslide. They arrest the owner of the M.O.C.K. Ock.

"My whole operation would have stayed secret except for that meddling kid and his weird dog," the man grumbles.

"The gang is going to love hearing about this adventure!" Shaggy says. "I wonder how many hot dogs this gold will buy?"

THE END

To follow another path, turn to page 11.

Velma waits on the beach for help. Other people run away from the sea monster. They stampede like a herd of frightened horses. Velma doesn't run. She isn't afraid. She and her friends have seen stranger creatures.

Velma knows she's in more danger from the frightened people than she is from the sea monster. The crowd tramples right over her. Velma is knocked to the ground. She can't get up.

"Hey! Watch where you're going!" Velma shouts. "Ow! Ow!"

Someone bumps into Velma, and her glasses go flying away. She can't see anything without them! Now she's afraid. Velma must decide what to do—and fast!

If Velma stays put on the sand, turn the page.
If Velma struggles to her feet, turn page 66.

Velma stays put on the sand. She can't see. Waves of people are running by her, nearly trampling her as they pass.

Then suddenly, she hears a familiar voice.

"Velma! You're safe!" Fred says. He grabs her wrist and pulls her to her feet.

"I found your glasses," Daphne says.

"Wow, am I glad to see you guys!" Velma exclaims as she puts on her glasses.

"It's a good thing I wasn't snorkeling when that thing showed up," Fred says. "I might have been monster food!"

"Speaking of food—where are Shaggy and Scooby-Doo?" asks Velma.

"I don't know," Daphne replies, looking around. "We'd better find them."

"I hope they're safe!" Velma says.

The screams of the frightened people running from the beach almost drown out a familiar voice. "Hey, guys! Over here!"

"Shaggy!" Velma shouts. She sees her friend trying to hide behind a big rock and wave at her at the same time.

Fred, Daphne, and Velma sprint toward the boulder. They make it to safety. Shaggy and Scooby-Doo shiver in fear behind the rock. The two pals hug each other as tight as suction cups.

"Scooby! Shaggy! Are you okay?" Daphne asks.

"R-ruh h-huh," Scooby-Doo stutters. "R-rat's a big r-ronster!"

"It might be big, but it's no monster," Velma declares.

"Whaaaat?" her friends say.

Turn to page 56.

Velma struggles to get to her feet. So many people are running over her! If she doesn't move, she'll be squished. Not only that, she'll never find her glasses.

Suddenly, Velma spots her glasses on the sand. And right beside them is the rarest of seashells, the Jewel of the Sea!

Velma studies its rainbow of colors and its delicate, spiral shape. She is so busy admiring the seashell that she doesn't see the huge tentacle coming right at her!

"Watch out!" yells a nearby lifeguard, trying to help her.

THWAP!

It's too late. The tentacle hits Velma and the lifeguard. Velma is knocked to the ground—again! The lifeguard falls on the sand next to her.

Velma gets up.

The lifeguard does not. He's unconscious.

"I guess I'll have to rescue *you*," Velma says. She drags the limp lifeguard toward a large rock.

The only thing on Velma's mind now is escape. The monster's tentacles whip around in the air. One of them slams down near Velma. It barely misses hitting her.

"Jeepers! That was close!" Velma says with a gasp. "Hey, go pick on someone your own size!"

A tentacle smashes the sand on Velma's left side. Another one crashes down on the right. Velma's back is up against the rock.

Right then, something grabs her from behind!

Turn to page 76.

"Ride? That's a great idea, pal!" Shaggy says. He heads for the nearest amusement park ride.

Shaggy and Scooby jump onto a spinning carousel. They try to hide among the animals and benches, but the sea monster isn't fooled.

The slimy sea creature spots them with its giant eye. One of its tentacles reaches for them.

"Rook out!" Scooby warns.

The tentacle grabs one of the carousel animals and uses it to spin the ride faster. The carousel goes around and around, faster and faster. The two pals can barely hang on.

FWOOSH! FWOOSH!

"Like, what do we do, Scoobs?" shouts Shaggy.

If Shaggy & Scooby hang on to the carousel, turn to page 69.
If Shaggy & Scooby let go of the ride, turn to page 43.

Shaggy and Scooby hang on tight. The carousel twirls like a spinning top.

Then, the sea monster stretches a tentacle and stops the ride suddenly. The pals fly off of the carousel, landing on their feet not far from the ride.

"Like, why's the ground moving?" Shaggy asks. He's very dizzy from the carousel.

Scooby-Doo runs around in circles. The canine can't stop himself from spinning. "I rink I'm gonna re rick!" he moans.

A giant tentacle grabs them. Shaggy and Scooby are too confused to escape.

They're doomed!

THE END

To follow another path, turn to page II.

Fred walks down the hallway. He tries to look like he belongs in the secret underwater stronghold. It works. No one pays any attention to him! Fred peeks into room after room. They are all barracks.

"No clues here," Fred decides. "There must be another level."

Fred finds stairs leading to an upper floor. He creeps up them cautiously. At the top he finds a huge room.

"Jackpot!" Fred says quietly. "This must be the mission planning room."

There are blueprints on the wall. They are designs of the mechanical sea monster. There are also maps of the U.S. coastlines and the locations of Navy bases.

"This is serious!" Fred realizes. "I've seen enough. It's time to get out of here."

Turn to page 53.

Daphne decides to steer the watercraft toward shore. She grounds the vehicle on the beach and helps Jacks off the passenger saddle.

They watch the sea monster wave its tentacles at the Coast Guard and police helicopters above. The show doesn't last very long. A Navy ship arrives and fires a net at the beast. It's a direct hit! The sea monster is trapped beneath the super-strong net very close to Daphne and Jacks.

"Well, that was impressive," Jacks says. "Almost as impressive as seeing a real, live sea monster."

"Oh, that was a fake," Daphne says. "I see these things all the time."

Jacks looks at Daphne, then at the trapped sea monster, then back at Daphne. He smiles his brilliant Hollywood smile.

"Impressive," he says.

Turn to page 96.

Shaggy and Scooby-Doo drop from the monster's grip. They don't fall far. Another tentacle grabs them. It's the same one holding Daphne, Fred, and Velma.

"Ri, guys!" Scooby says.

"Scooby-Doo, you're brilliant!" Fred exclaims. "You've given me an idea."

"Rho, me? Hee hee hee!" Scooby giggles.

"When Scooby bit that tentacle, it shorted out. The monster is a fake," Fred says. "We have to short out this tentacle."

"It'll open up and let us go, too," Velma realizes. "That's a great plan, Fred."

"Go for it, pal!" Shaggy says.

Scooby-Doo chomps down on the tentacle.

CLANG! ZAP!

There is a bright flash of light and energy.

Turn the page.

Sparks fly everywhere. Instead of letting go of the kids, the tentacle conducts a huge electrical shock from tip to base and back again.

"Yaaa!" they yell. Their hair stands on end.

Suddenly, the mechanical monster stops in its tracks. The shock has blown out all its controls.

"You did it, Scoob!" Shaggy shouts. "You must have hit a nerve!"

The sea monster is not able to stand up. It starts to tip over.

"Ruh-oh," Scooby realizes. "Ris isn't rood."

The monster falls into the water with a tremendous splash! The gang swims away from the wreckage. So does the man controlling the monster.

"You meddling kids destroyed my plan!" he shouts at the gang. Nearby police officers pull him from the water.

"I wanted to scare people away from the park," he continues. "My rival owns it, and I wanted to ruin him. I would have gotten away with it, too, if it hadn't been for you!"

"Maybe the park owner can turn that monster machine into a real ride," Shaggy says. "It was kind of fun!"

THE END

To follow another path, turn to page 11.

Something that doesn't feel human wraps around Velma and pulls her. She fights against it! She holds onto the unconscious lifeguard. The weight of his limp body is like an anchor. Velma doesn't know which is worse—the sea monster's tentacles in front of her or the unknown menace behind her.

"Hey, Velma! It's us!" Shaggy says.

"Ryeah! Rit's us!" Scooby-Doo says. "Re're trying to save rou!"

Velma sees that it's Scooby's paws wrapped around her. He pulls her and the lifeguard behind the big boulder.

"Like, that's a seriously serious sea monster!" Shaggy exclaims. "Where'd it come from?"

Velma barely has time to think about that question. A giant tentacle picks up the rock. There's no place to hide!

"Zoinks! Like, run!" Shaggy shouts.

Scooby's legs spin like a crazy windmill. So do Shaggy's! The pals are so scrambled that they run into each other and fall flat on the sand.

"Whoa! Talk about going nowhere, fast," Shaggy says.

"Ri see stars!" Scooby-Doo says, giggling. "Ris rat the Rig Dipper?"

SMASH! The tentacle throws the boulder to the ground. It misses Velma and her friends by inches. The impact wakes up the lifeguard.

"Earthquake!" he yells.

"Nope. Not even close," Velma says. Another tentacle crashes down. "Let's get out of here!"

The group runs toward the pier. They'll be safe under the timber supports. But the monster comes up out of the water and chases them!

Turn to page 80.

Fred raises his hands in surrender. "I'm not a bad guy," he says. "I'm just wearing one of their wet suits!"

Fred tells the Coast Guard officer about the underwater HQ and the secret planning room he discovered. The officer's expression turns intense. "Take this kid to the brig!" he orders.

"But . . . but!" Fred stutters. He is escorted below decks to a steel cell. Bars clang shut. "I'm doomed."

"I'm a condemned prisoner," Fred moans inside his cell. "If I were Shaggy or Scooby, I'd know what I'd want for my last meal. Everything!"

Later, a Coast Guard officer comes into the brig and unlocks the cell door. "You're free to go," he tells Fred.

As Fred leaves, he sees a group of men in handcuffs.

"Is that the meddling kid who ruined our plans?" one of them shouts. "We would have gotten away with it if it hadn't been for you!"

"They're international spies," the officer tells Fred. "Thanks for telling us their location. You're a hero."

"Wow! I can't wait to tell the gang about this!" Fred says. "Who knew snorkeling could be so exciting?"

THE END

To follow another path, turn to page 11.

Velma risks looking back at the monster. She sees something strange. It has mechanical legs! They have been hidden under water until now.

"The monster is a machine!" Velma shouts. Her friends stop and look. "It might look like a monster on top, but the bottom is man-made."

"That's great to know, Velma—but it's still chasing us!" says Shaggy.

"I have an idea how to stop it," Velma says. She points to a dune buggy parked near the pier.

"Like, this is no time for a joyride, Velma," Shaggy says.

Velma hops into the dune buggy. Her friends are astonished to see her drive straight at the sea monster! She zooms under its legs. The tentacles try to grab her but they get tangled in the legs. The monster ties itself in knots.

Suddenly, it tips over and falls onto the sand!

Turn to page 82.

"Help! Help!" someone cries. The sound comes from inside the monster.

The lifeguard runs up to the monster's head. He pulls out one of its eyes.

"Ewww!" Scooby says.

"There's someone inside!" the lifeguard says. "I have to save—her?"

He lifts a beautiful woman out of the mechanical monster.

"Thank you!" she exclaims. "I'm a stunt driver, and this machine went out of control."

"You're safe now," the lifeguard says as he carries her toward the first-aid station.

"Hey, for once the monster was a damsel in distress!" Shaggy says.

THE END

To follow another path, turn to page 11.

Daphne heads farther out to sea.

A giant tentacle smashes down in the water in front of them. It creates a wave that almost tips over the watercraft. Daphne and Jacks hold on for their lives.

"Well, I guess we can't outrun this creepy creature," Jacks decides.

Daphne quickly turns the watercraft in the opposite direction. Another tentacle blocks any chance of escape.

"Aw, come on!" shouts Jacks.

"I'll try to get to those rocks," Daphne suggests. She points to a pile of boulders that are part of a fishing jetty. "We can hide there."

"If we can get there," Jacks says.

VA-ROOM! Daphne presses the accelerator.

"This would be a great action movie, but I don't much like it in real life," Jacks says.

Turn the page.

Daphne steers the watercraft in crazy zigzags to avoid the monster's tentacles.

"We're almost out of danger!" Daphne says, speeding toward the rocks a few yards away.

"Full speed ahead!" Jacks shouts in triumph.

Suddenly, a huge shadow blocks out the sun above their heads. Daphne and Jacks look up and see a giant tentacle descending toward them.

There's no escape from this one!

"Jump!" Daphne yells. She and Jacks leap off the watercraft.

SPA-LOOOSH!

They land in the water with a big splash. The watercraft crashes into the rocks just as the tentacle smashes down on it.

There is a loud explosion!

KA-BOOM!

"That was close!" Jacks exclaims as he floats on the surface. He swims over to Daphne. "Are you all right?"

"I am, but the monster isn't. Look!" Daphne observes. She points to the monster. "It's on fire!"

"I don't know much about sea monsters, but are they usually this flammable?" Jacks asks.

"They are if they're fake," Daphne replies. "It's a machine!"

The flames burn away layers of plastic and foam on the monster, exposing a steel skeleton. Fiery debris lands near Daphne and Jacks.

"Let's get to shore," Jacks suggests. They swim along the jetty to the beach.

Once on dry land, they watch the monster burn, spark, and explode.

Pieces of the mechanical menace fly through the air.

Turn the page.

"This is more exciting than the Fourth of July," Jacks says. A chunk of burning debris lands close by. "Although it might be a tad dangerous."

"Sometimes I think 'Danger' should be my middle name," Daphne remarks. "Daphne 'Danger' Blake."

"Pleased to meet you, Daphne," Jacks replies. "Formal introductions at last."

Turn to page 96.

The mechanical monster tightens its grip on the robot mascot. Shaggy desperately tries to find a way to break free. He hits every button on the control panel. Suddenly, the mascot starts to walk backward. Then it begins to fall! The sea monster can't let go in time. Both machines tip over and crash into the surf!

Shaggy and Scooby climb out of the robot mascot. Velma, Daphne, and Fred run up to them. Nearby, the man in the sea monster crawls out of the wreckage.

"You meddling kid!" he grumbles as the police arrest him. "I was chasing everyone away so I could dig up the pirate treasure under the pier."

"Like, thanks for the tip," Shaggy says with a smile. "Now I can pay for the mascot I just broke!"

THE END

To follow another path, turn to page II.

Daphne's kite is cut to ribbons, tearing apart in midair. Daphne drops like a stone and hits the water with a splash. The shredded kite floats down from above and settles on top of her. The fabric soaks up the seawater and becomes very heavy. It starts to drag her down!

"I'd better get out from under this kite or I'll end up on the bottom," Daphne says. She tries to swim through one of the rips in the canopy but the kite lines are twisted around her legs. She can barely move. "I'm trapped!"

Daphne begins to sink!

"Hello, miss. Need a hand?" a nearby voice says. Daphne is under the kite canopy and can't see who it is. It doesn't matter to her. She needs help—and fast!

"Yes, please," Daphne replies. "I'm tangled in my kite lines."

"That's an easy fix," the voice declares.

RIIIIP!

This time, the tearing sound is good news. The kite's fabric is cut away, and Daphne is saved from drowning. She looks up at her rescuer and almost chokes.

"You . . . you," Daphne sputters in surprise.

"Take it easy, miss. I've got you," the rescuer says. He reaches down and grabs her wrist to keep her from sinking.

Daphne recognizes him. He's one of the celebrities she wanted to see at the beach!

"Thank you, sir," Daphne says shyly.

The famous actor takes a pocketknife and cuts the kite lines tangled around her legs. "Sir? Please! Call me Jacks. It's short for—" he starts.

"I know," Daphne blurts as he lifts her onto the watercraft. "Hold on, I'm driving."

Turn the page.

"Right then. Formal introductions later," Jacks says, taking his place on the back of the watercraft. "It looks like there's a sea monster menacing the good people of Wild-World Beach. I've been in loads of action films, but I've never seen the likes of this before!"

"I see this sort of thing all the time," Daphne says, sighing.

Jacks doesn't hear her over the roar of the watercraft's engine.

FWOOOOSH!

"Head farther out to sea!" shouts Jacks. "We can outrun this creepy creature."

"Don't you think we should head to shore instead?" says Daphne, punching the accelerator. "We'll be safer on land."

"The choice is yours," says Jacks.

If Daphne heads toward shore, turn to page 72.
If Daphne heads farther out to sea, turn to page 83.

The room is filled with treasure! There are golden plates hanging on the wall and a shoulder-high pile of jewels in a corner. Next to it is a stack of silver-plated armor and a pot of gold coins. Fred is stunned by the sight.

"Wow!" Fred exclaims. "This isn't a spaceship, it's a treasure hunt!"

"Hey, you! What are you doing in here?" a man shouts. It's one of the treasure hunters.

Fred doesn't reply. He runs!

Fred tries to get back to the docking bay. He wants to use one of the sea monster subs to make his escape. Guards block his path. Desperate, Fred locks himself in the maintenance room. It's full of pipes and machinery.

"I need a plan!" Fred says. "I need to distract the guards so I can escape. But how?"

Suddenly, Fred sees the solution. There is a thick steel door labeled Emergency Exit.

"Well, this is an emergency and I need an exit," Fred shrugs. He turns the large metal wheel on the hatch. "I just hope I can get this open!"

SPLOOOOSH!

The door flies open with a tremendous gush of water. Electrical systems blow up and the lights go out! Fred takes a deep breath and swims.

Turn to page 105.

Shaggy and Scooby-Doo run through the amusement park trying to hide from the sea monster. It doesn't give up the chase. Its tentacles whip the air trying to grab them.

"We're doomed!" Shaggy says.

"Ri'm too roung to rie!" Scooby moans.

The pals flee from the monster past the carousel and the waterslide, past the roller coaster and the Ferris wheel. Then they do it again. And again.

Like, weren't we just here? Shaggy wonders.

Suddenly, there is nowhere else to run. They've reached the end of the amusement park.

"Zoinks! We're at the end of the pier," Shaggy says. Waves crash against the dangerous rocks below. "We're trapped!"

"Roh no re're not!" Scooby-Doo declares. He grabs his friend and jumps!

Turn to page 59.

A man climbs out of the sea monster that brought Fred to the ship. He goes through a doorway. Fred decides to follow. He disguises himself in a maintenance jumpsuit and grabs a rusted toolbox.

No one notices Fred as he wanders through the so-called spaceship. He discovers bedrooms, a cafeteria, and a maintenance room, but nothing reveals the purpose of the place. Then Fred comes to a door labeled Treasure Room.

"What kind of treasure?" Fred wonders. He peeks inside. *GASP!*

Fred can barely believe his eyes!

Turn to page 92.

From the beach, Daphne and Jacks watch the sea monster break apart. The creature is made of metal and plastic. Daphne was right about it being a fake.

"This would make a great action movie," Jacks says. "Starring me, of course."

"My life is an action movie!" Daphne laughs. "And if there's one thing I've learned, it's that there are no *real* monsters."

"Daphne! Are you all right?" Velma shouts as she and the rest of the gang run toward her.

"We saw your kiteboard and then that monster!" Fred says.

"Fake monster," Daphne tells her friends.

"Like, not again. Why can't we have a normal day at the beach?" Shaggy says.

"I might have to reconsider the definition of normal," Jacks comments.

A man staggers out of the surf near Jacks and the gang. "My monster. My beautiful monster— ruined!" he cries. Then he sees Scooby and the gang standing nearby. "You meddling kids, it's all your fault!"

"What did we do?" Velma protests.

"Like, we just got here," Shaggy adds.

"You're the one driving a giant machine around and scaring people," Daphne points out.

"This bloke must have knocked his noggin. His reasoning is all out of whack," Jacks says. He waves at a squad of police driving down the beach. They quickly arrest the crazy culprit.

"I wonder why that bloke built that monster?" Jacks says as the police drive away. "Why threaten people? What did he have to gain?"

"Revenge, greed, jealousy, a childhood rivalry," Daphne counts on her fingers.

Turn the page.

"We've seen just about everything, haven't we, gang?" Daphne asks.

"Ryeah!" Scooby agrees.

"You've got a talking dog?!" Jacks exclaims. "Now I've seen everything!"

"Scooby-Doo is one-of-a-kind," Daphne says.

"I could say the same about you," Jacks tells Daphne with a Hollywood smile. "Why don't we have dinner? I know a great seafood place."

"I'd love to!" Daphne replies.

The gang watches Jacks and Daphne walk down the beach arm-in-arm.

"Well, Daphne got her celebrity sighting!" Velma remarks.

"And dinner, too!" Shaggy sighs. "Lucky girl!"

THE END

To follow another path, turn to page 11.

Shaggy and Scooby investigate the screams.

"Wow! It sounds like people are having a lot of fun," Shaggy says. "They sure are yelling!"

"Rook! Rit's a ride!" Scooby shouts. He points to a giant sea monster in the water. There are people in its tentacles screaming their lungs out.

"It must be new. Groovy!" Shaggy says. "Let's check it out!"

The pals run down to the beach to get on the ride. The beach is empty.

"Hey, like, we're in luck, Scoob. There's no line!" Shaggy says with a laugh.

"How do re get on?" Scooby asks.

Suddenly, a large tentacle reaches out and grabs Scooby and Shaggy. They are carried high into the air!

"Cool! Automatic pickup!" Shaggy exclaims. "Like, this is real high-tech."

Turn to page 101.

They see Daphne, Fred, and Velma in one of the tentacles, screaming and waving wildly at them. Shaggy waves back. He and Scooby are happy on the ride—until the tentacle starts to squeeze too tight.

"Hey, that hurts. Who's running this ride?" Shaggy gasps.

"Gulp! Ris is a real rea monster!" Scooby says.

Shaggy realizes his friends are screaming in fear, not amusement. He starts screaming, too. Scooby opens his mouth to yell, but the hungry hound has another thought.

"Seafood," he says and chomps on the tentacle.

CLANG! Scooby's teeth hit metal. The monster is mechanical! *ZAP!* Sparks fly from the tentacle. It opens up and releases Shaggy and Scooby.

If Shaggy & Scooby fall to the water, turn to page 35.
If Shaggy & Scooby twist in more tentacles, turn to page 73.

Velma grabs the door handle on the left.

"I can't believe it!" she exclaims. "The door is unlocked! Whoever invented this sea monster forgot basic security."

A metal staircase winds up to another door at the top. Velma sprints up the steps. This time, she doesn't hesitate to open the door.

Velma bursts into the mechanical monster's high-tech control room. The man at the controls is startled to see her.

"I thought I locked that door!" he shouts.

"I don't know anything about your evil scheme, but you're not getting away with it," Velma declares.

"You've got one thing right—you don't know anything," the man replies. "What do you know about designing an extraterrestrial terrain vehicle for the space program?"

"Well, a lot, actually," Velma starts to say.

"Nothing!" the man says, not listening to her answer. "My designs were perfect, and I still got fired from the program."

"Jeepers, I wonder why," Velma replies.

"This prototype was supposed to explore strange new worlds, to walk on alien soil," the man continues.

"Uh, so why is it in the ocean right now?" Velma asks. She doesn't really want an answer, but she wants to keep the man distracted. She needs time to study the control panel.

Suddenly, Velma spots the key to stopping the mad inventor's monster!

Velma realizes that the monster might be big and scary, but the controls to this machine are simple and easy. She'll just need to reach the key located on the main panel.

Turn the page.

"It's just like an ignition key that starts a car—or turns it off!" Velma realizes. The teen leaps for the key and switches it off. The mechanical monster slows to a halt.

"Hey! You can't do that!" the man shouts.

Velma doesn't reply. She grabs the key and runs out of the control room. She goes down the stairs and back to the room with the hatch. The hatch is open!

"Geronimo!" Velma shouts as she jumps out of the metal monster and into the water.

Police boats rush toward the monster.

"Another mystery solved," Velma says. "The gang is going to love this one!"

THE END

To follow another path, turn to page 11.

Fred follows the faint glow of sunlight to the surface. He looks around to see how far from shore he is. All he can see are fake alien guards treading water nearby. "That's him!" one of them shouts, pointing at Fred. "That's the meddling kid who flooded our hideout!"

"We were almost finished uncovering the buried treasure. We would have gotten away if you hadn't interfered!" another crook says angrily.

"Get him!" a guard yells.

The guards and crooks swim toward Fred. Suddenly, a pod of dolphins surfaces and comes between Fred and the hunters.

"Thanks, pals!" Fred says as the dolphins carry him to safety. "When we get to shore I'll introduce you to my friend, Scooby-Doo!"

THE END

To follow another path, turn to page 11.

AUTHOR

Laurie S. Sutton has read comics since she was a kid. She grew up to become an editor for Marvel, DC Comics, Starblaze, and Tekno Comics. She has written Adam Strange for DC, Star Trek: Voyager for Marvel, plus Star Trek: Deep Space Nine and Witch Hunter for Malibu Comics. There are long boxes of comics in her closet where there should be clothing and shoes. Laurie has lived all over the world. She currently resides in Florida.

ILLUSTRATOR

Scott Neely has been a professional illustrator and designer for many years. For the last eight years, he's been an official Scooby-Doo and Cartoon Network artist, working on such licensed properties as Dexter's Laboratory, Johnny Bravo, Courage the Cowardly Dog, Powerpuff Girls, and more. He has also worked on Pokémon, Mickey Mouse Clubhouse, My Friends Tigger & Pooh, Handy Manny, Strawberry Shortcake, Bratz, and many other popular characters. He lives in a suburb of Philadelphia and has a scrappy Yorkshire Terrier, Alfie.

GLOSSARY

beacon (BEE-kuhn)—a light or fire used as a signal or warning

extraterrestrial (ek-struh-tuh-RESS-tree-uhl)—coming from outer space

geyser (GYE-zur)—a hole in the ground through which hot water and steam shoot up in bursts

maritime (MA-ri-tym)—of, relating to, or near the sea

meddling (MED-uhl-ing)—interfering in someone else's business

moored (MOORD)—tied up or anchored, as a ship

parallel (PA-ruh-lel)—lying or moving in the same direction but always the same distance apart

phony (FO-nee)—not genuine or real

reef (REEF)—a strip of rock, sand, or coral close to the surface of the ocean or another body of water

snorkel (SNOR-kuhl)—to swim underwater using a tube for breathing

temptation (temp-TAY-shuhn)—something you want to have or do, although you know it's wrong

unconscious (uhn-KON-shuhss)—not awake or able to see, feel, or think

YOU CHOOSE JOKES!

YOU CHOOSE which punch line is funniest!

Why does the sea monster eat lunch by the shore?

a. Because of all the sand which is (sandwiches) on the beach!

b. Because he can't fit in the pool!

c. Because the islands weren't Philippine him up, so he needed Samoa to eat!

What happened when Scooby-Doo accidentally swallowed his flashlight?

a. He barked with de light!

b. Shaggy said, "There he glows!"

c. He was still hungry because it was only a light snack.

Why did the sea monster cross the ocean?

a. To get to the other tide!

b. To sleep in his own seabed.

c. He heard he'd get plenty of mussels on the trip.

Why did the lobster rush out of the bathroom?
a. He won't say why. He just clams up!
b. Because the sardines were filling up the can!
c. Because he wanted to use the paper towels, but he ran out!

What was the ghost wearing when it chased Scooby-Doo?
a. Boo jeans!
b. A boo tie!
c. It was driving a car so it wore a sheet belt!

Why do seagulls fly over the sea?
a. If they flew over the bay they would be called bagels!
b. If they flew over a football field they'd be field gulls!
c. If they flew over the North Pole they'd be icicles (icy gulls)!

What does Scooby-Doo wear during the summer?
a. He wears his coat and pants!
b. Rightweight crows!
c. Nothing, he likes hot dogs!